This book belongs to:

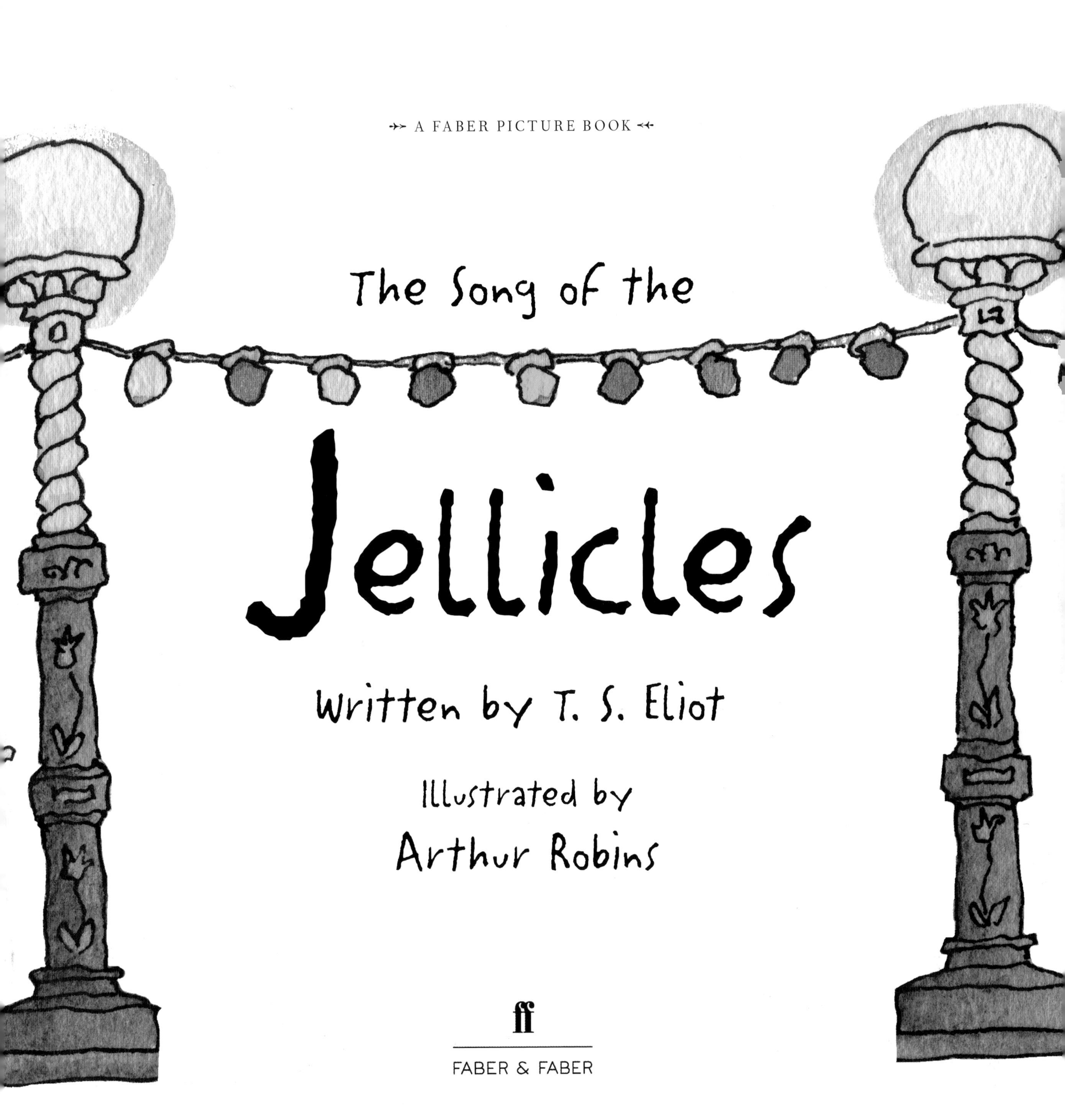

A FABER PICTURE BOOK

The Song of the Jellicles

Written by T. S. Eliot

Illustrated by Arthur Robins

ff

FABER & FABER

Jellicle Cats come out to-night
Jellicle Cats come one come all:

The Jellicle Moon is shining bright—
Jellicles come to the Jellicle Ball.

Jellicle Cats are
black and white,

Jellicle Cats
are rather
small;

Jellicle Cats
are merry
and bright,

And pleasant
to hear when
they caterwaul.

Jellicle Cats have
cheerful faces,

Jellicle Cats have
bright black eyes;

They like to practise their airs and graces

And wait for the
Jellicle Moon to rise.

Jellicle Cats develop slowly,
Jellicle Cats are not too big;

Jellicle Cats are roly-poly,
They know how to dance a gavotte and a jig.

Until the Jellicle Moon appears
They make their
toilette and take
their repose:
Jellicles wash
behind their ears,

Jellicles dry
between
their toes.

Jellicle Cats are white and black,
Jellicle Cats are of moderate size;

Jellicles jump like a jumping-jack,

Jellicle Cats have moonlit eyes.

They're quiet enough in the morning hours,

They're quiet enough in the afternoon,
Reserving their terpsichorean powers

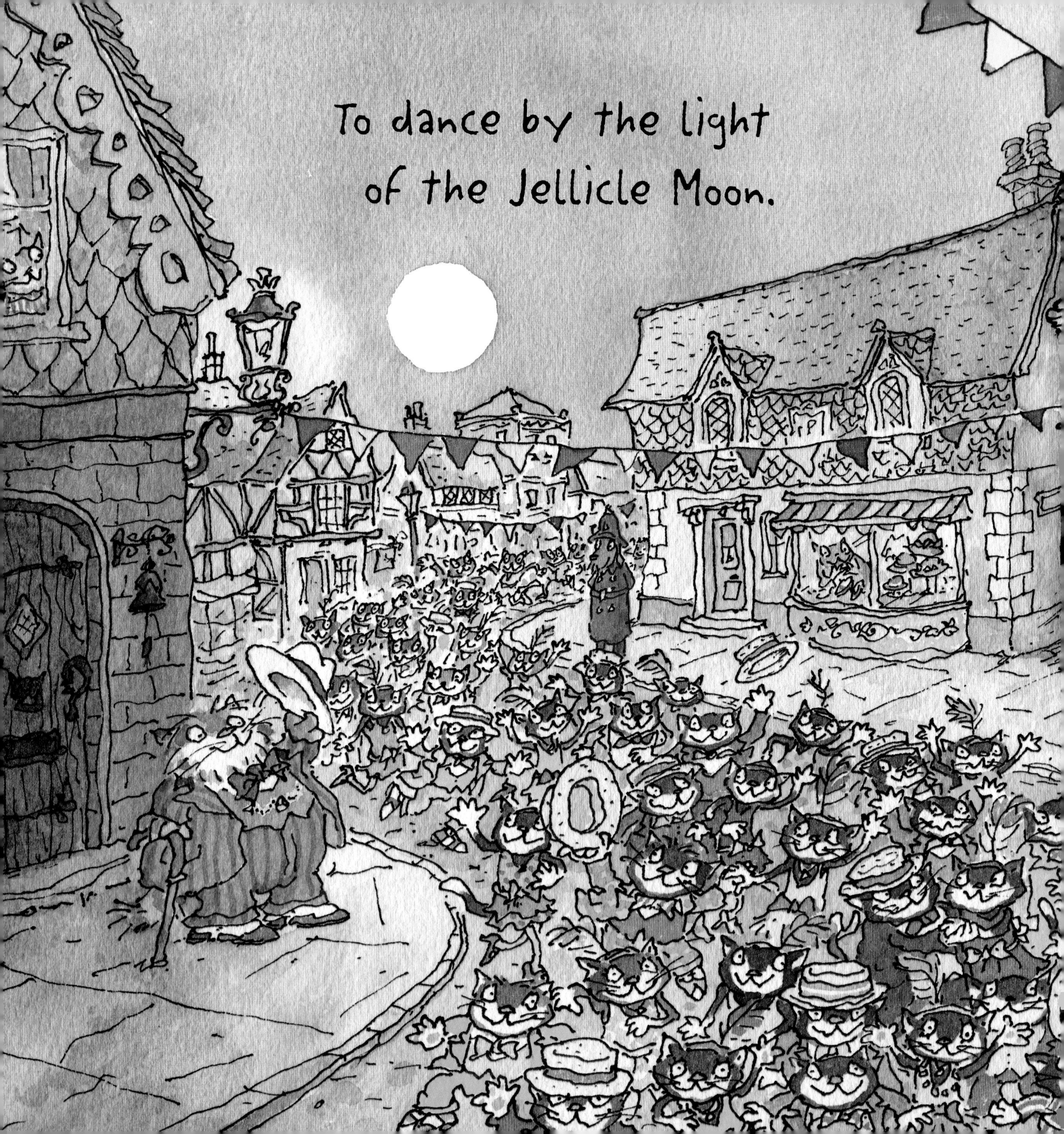
To dance by the light
of the Jellicle Moon.

Jellicle Cats are black and white,
Jellicle Cats (as I said) are small;

If it happens to be a stormy night

They will practise a
caper or two in the hall.
If it happens the sun
is shining bright

You would say they had
nothing to do at all:

They are resting and saving
themselves to be right

For the Jellicle Moon
and the Jellicle Ball.

From the original collection,
'respectfully dedicated to those friends who have assisted its composition by their encouragement, criticism and suggestions: and in particular to Mr T. E. Faber, Miss Alison Tandy, Miss Susan Wolcott, Miss Susanna Morley, and the Man in White Spats. O.P.'

First published in 1939 in *Old Possum's Book of Practical Cats*
by Faber and Faber Ltd,
Bloomsbury House, 74—77 Great Russell Street, London WC1b 3DA
This edition first published in 2017

Printed in China

Design by Ness Wood

A CIP record for this book is available from the British Library
ISBN 978—0—571—33341—7

2 4 6 8 10 9 7 5 3 1